D0582448

THE STORY OF
MISS MOPPET

THE STORY OF
MISS MOPPET

BY

BEATRIX POTTER

Author of
" *The Tale of Peter Rabbit,*" *etc.*

LONDON
FREDERICK WARNE & CO., Ltd.
AND NEW YORK

(*All rights reserved*)

*Copyright in all countries
signatory to the Berne Convention*
FREDERICK WARNE & CO. LTD.
LONDON, ENGLAND.

ORD EDN ISBN 0 7232 0612 0
LIB EDN ISBN 0 7232 0635 X

PRINTED IN GREAT BRITAIN FOR THE PUBLISHERS
BY HENRY STONE AND SON (PRINTERS) LTD., BANBURY
205.475

THIS is a Pussy called
Miss Moppet, she thinks
she has heard a mouse !

THIS is the Mouse peeping
out behind the cup-
board, and making fun of
Miss Moppet. He is not
afraid of a kitten.

11

12

THIS is Miss Moppet
jumping just too late ;
she misses the Mouse and
hits her own head.

S HE thinks it is a very
   hard cupboard !

15

16

THE Mouse watches Miss
    Moppet from the top of
the cupboard.

MISS MOPPET ties up
her head in a duster,
and sits before the fire.

19

THE Mouse thinks she is looking very ill. He comes sliding down the bell-pull.

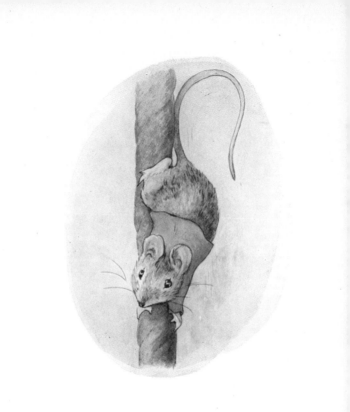

21

MISS MOPPET looks
worse and worse. The
Mouse comes a little nearer.

MISS MOPPET holds
her poor head in her
paws, and looks at him
through a hole in the duster.
The Mouse comes *very* close.

A ND then all of a sudden
— Miss Moppet jumps
upon the Mouse !

AND because the Mouse has teased Miss Moppet — Miss Moppet thinks she will tease the Mouse; which is not at all nice of Miss Moppet.

S HE ties him up in the
duster, and tosses it
about like a ball.

BUT she forgot about that hole in the duster ; and when she untied it — there was no Mouse !

HE has wriggled out and run away; and he is dancing a jig on the top of the cupboard!